DANGEROUS
GAMES
LOCKDOWN

Sue Graves

Rising Stars UK Ltd.
7 Hatchers Mews, Bermondsey Street, London SE1 3GS
www.risingstars-uk.com

 nasen

NASEN House, 4/5 Amber Business Village, Amber Close,
Amington, Tamworth, Staffordshire B77 4RP

Published 2012

Author: Sue Graves
Series editor: Sasha Morton
Text and logo design: pentacor**big**
Typesetting: Geoff Rayner, Bag of Badgers
Cover design: Lon Chan
Publisher: Gill Budgell
Project Manager: Sasha Morton Creative Project Management
Editorial: Deborah Kespert
Artwork: Colour: Lon Chan / B&W: Paul Loudon

British Library Cataloguing in Publication Data.
A CIP record for this book is available from the British Library.

ISBN: 978-0-85769-613-7

Printed by Craftprint International, Singapore

It was Wednesday evening and Tom, Sima and Kojo were at a special jewel exhibition at the City Gallery. Kojo's cousin, Jasmine, was the curator there and she had given them free tickets for the event. Tom and Kojo looked very smart in their dinner jackets and Sima looked beautiful in a long gold dress. Round her neck she wore a sparkling crystal on a thin, silver chain. Tom and Kojo had given it to her for her birthday and she loved it.

Sima, Tom and Kojo worked at Dangerous Games, a computer games company. Sima designed the games, Kojo programmed them and Tom tested them. They worked as a team and they were all good mates.

"This is such a cool place," said Tom taking a canapé. "The food tastes great!"

"Yeah," said Kojo. "There are some great people here, too." He nodded towards a group of people on the other side of the gallery. "Look, there's that guy from the band, Dudes Rule."

"Where?" asked Sima excitedly.

"There," said Kojo, pointing across the room.

"Ooh yes," said Sima. "He's really cool. I wonder if I could get his autograph."

Tom rolled his eyes. "That's so sad!" he said.

Just then, Kojo's cousin came over to speak to them.

"Enjoying yourselves, folks?" she asked.

"You bet," said Sima. "This is a fantastic evening. The jewellery in the exhibition is gorgeous, too."

"And so is the food," said Tom as he took another canapé from a passing waiter.

Jasmine laughed. "I'm glad you're having fun."

"What's the most expensive piece of jewellery here?" asked Sima.

"Ah, yes!" said Jasmine. "We have a really special jewel here tonight. Come with me and I'll show you."

Sima, Tom and Kojo followed Jasmine into
a small room off the main gallery. There in
the middle of the floor was a glass case with
spotlights shining onto it from every angle. Inside
the case was a large orange gem. It flashed and
sparkled in the bright light.

"What sort of stone is that?" asked Sima,
looking puzzled. "I don't recognise it, but it looks
amazing."

THE FIRE DIAMOND

"It is amazing," said Jasmine. "It's a very special and extremely rare orange diamond. It's called 'The Fire Diamond' because it is such a deep shade of orange. When the light catches it, it looks as if it's on fire."

"Wow!" breathed Sima, bending down to get a closer look.

Tom grinned and tapped the glass case. "I hope your security's good," he laughed, "or else Sima might run off with the stone."

"She wouldn't get far," said Jasmine. "Our security measures are the best. No one would be able to steal this diamond."

"Can I take a photo of it?" asked Kojo, pulling out his phone.

"Be my guest," said Jasmine. "It's the closest you'll ever get to it!"

Later on, as they walked home, Tom, Sima and Kojo talked about the exhibition.

"That was brilliant," said Kojo.

"It was fantastic," said Sima. "I felt like a millionaire dressed up in my best dress and looking at all that fabulous jewellery. I just wish I could own something as amazing as the Fire Diamond."

"Your crystal cost me and Kojo a fortune," said Tom. "Unless we win the lottery, you won't be getting anything as expensive as a Fire Diamond from us."

"Cheapskates!" laughed Sima.

Kojo walked ahead deep in thought.

"What are you thinking about?" called Sima.

"I bet loads of thieves would be keen to get their hands on that diamond," said Kojo. "I wonder if it might be an idea for a new game."

"How do you mean?" asked Tom.

"Well," explained Kojo, "the game could be set in the City Gallery. A gang of thieves could try to steal the diamond."

"Yes," said Sima looking excited, "and the players could control the game from the security room at the gallery. They would have to make sure all the security devices were deployed in time to stop the thieves from stealing the diamond. You've given me some great ideas, Kojo. I'll start work on them in the morning."

CHAPTER 2

The next morning Sima set to work on the designs for the new jewel thief game. Tom downloaded information about security devices from the internet for her. Sima included lots of them in the game. Before long, the designs were finished.

"Our game has more security devices than the City Gallery," boasted Sima. "No thief can get past all of these!"

Once Sima had double-checked the designs, Kojo programmed the game and soon it was ready for Tom to test.

"Let's test this game for real," said Tom.

"I can't see the point of that," said Sima. "The game's foolproof. The players will always win, because no thief can possibly beat my brilliant devices."

"Maybe," said Tom. "But don't you think it would be fun to play it for real? It would be a really good laugh."

"Well … I suppose so," said Sima doubtfully.

"Great," said Tom. "It's agreed. We'll play it after work." As soon as everyone else at Dangerous Games had gone home for the night, Tom, Sima and Kojo got ready to play the game.

"Now remember," Kojo said, "we must all touch the screen at the same time to enter the game. As usual, it's only finished when we hear the words 'Game Over'. Understood?"

"Understood!"

Kojo loaded the game and they all touched the screen. They shut their eyes tightly as a bright light flashed. Then the light faded and they opened their eyes.

CHAPTER 3

Sima, Tom and Kojo found themselves in the security room at the City Gallery.

"This is brilliant," said Tom. "Look at all these controls." He began to flick a few of the switches.

"Don't Tom!" warned Sima. "You can only use the controls when the thieves enter the game. I hope you haven't messed things up."

"Of course I haven't," said Tom, and he quickly flicked the switches back again.

Kojo sat down in front of a bank of screens. They showed every part of the gallery — it looked as if everything was OK.

Just then, Tom spotted a movement in one of the rooms. "What was that?" he said. "I think the game has started for real. I'm sure I saw a shadow across the back wall. Zoom the camera in closer, Kojo."

Kojo zoomed in the CCTV camera.

LOOK, THERE!

Crouching down in the gloom were two men. They were dressed all in black and wore balaclavas over their heads. Suddenly, the camera seemed to rock and the screen in the security room went blank.

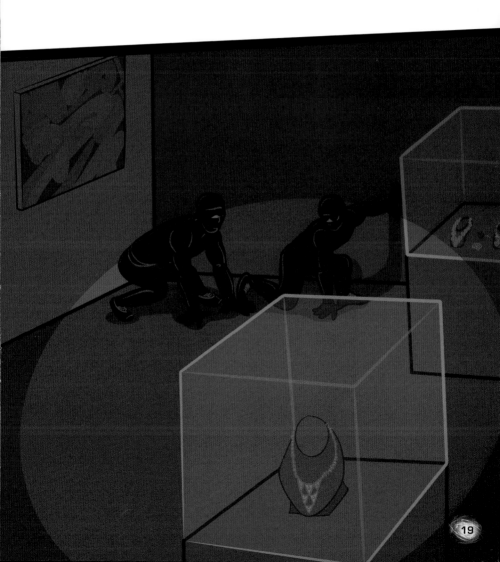

Kojo checked the switches but nothing worked. "I think we must have more than two thieves," he said. "Someone has disabled the camera in that room and it couldn't have been done by the two men we could see. They were nowhere near the camera when it went down."

"Check the other screens!" shouted Sima. "We've got to keep track of the thieves or else they will get the diamond."

Tom and Kojo checked the other screens. It looked as if everything was in order but suddenly they spotted the men hiding near the doorway to the room where the diamond was.

"How did they get there so quickly?" asked Sima. "They've bypassed several devices already." She glared at Tom. "This is all your fault," she snapped. "You shouldn't have messed around with those switches when we first started the game."

ACTIVATE THE LASERS. THEY WON'T BE ABLE TO SPOT THOSE.

"Instead of arguing," interrupted Kojo, "let's stay in control of the situation. The thieves are just outside the room where the diamond is. Which security device do you want us to activate?"

Tom activated the lasers. They could see the red lines criss-crossing the floor. The thieves were standing in the doorway. Suddenly, they began somersaulting through the lasers. They didn't trigger a single one.

THAT'S JUST NOT POSSIBLE! HOW COULD THEY HAVE KNOWN THE LASERS WERE THERE?

Kojo zoomed in the CCTV camera for a closer look at the thieves. "Look!" he said. "They've put on some sort of special glasses. The glasses must show them where the lasers are. No wonder they can get past them."

"This is looking serious," said Tom. "The thieves are in the room where the diamond is. They're making for the glass case."

Sima grinned. "It doesn't matter if they do," she said. "I've designed a fake diamond to look just like the real thing. The one you can see in the glass case is made from paste."

"Neat!" said Tom. He looked at the time on his watch. "This is going to be easy. The thieves aren't even close to getting the real diamond."

Just then, the thieves stopped. One of the men shone a blue light at the fake diamond. He kicked the case angrily and shouted at the other men.

"Oh no," said Sima, "I think we've been found out. That guy knows the diamond is a fake."

"So where's the real diamond?" asked Kojo.

"I've hidden it in a small safe in the back room of the gallery," explained Sima. "They shouldn't find it there."

I WOULDN'T BE SO SURE.

But the men ran into the back room and began looking behind all the pictures on the wall for a safe.

"Time for another of your security devices," said Tom. "What can we activate now?"

Sima looked worried. "That's it. There are no more devices. The thieves will find the safe any second now."

CHAPTER 4

Tom, Sima and Kojo ran down the stairs and crept into the gallery. They could hear the thieves in the back room.

"What can we do?" whispered Sima. "If they find the safe and crack the code they'll be seconds away from grabbing the diamond."

Kojo pulled out his phone and began pressing the buttons as fast as he could.

"You're not phoning the police, are you?" asked Sima. "By the time they get here the thieves will be long gone and so will the Fire Diamond."

"No, I'm not phoning the police," said Kojo. "But I've got an idea." He scanned through the photos on his phone. "Look," he said. "Here's the photo I took of the diamond."

"What use is that at a time like this?" asked Tom.

"I've got an app on my phone that converts photos into holograms," explained Kojo. "I'm going to add a picture of an open safe and cut and paste the hologram of the diamond into it to recreate exactly what the thieves are looking for."

Kojo pressed a button on his phone and holograms of the diamond in an open safe appeared all round the back room.

The thieves looked startled. They ran from one hologram to another and soon they were arguing loudly.

"This is brilliant," whispered Sima. "But the true diamond is still not safe. Look!"

The thieves were getting closer and closer to the
real safe and the real diamond!

"It's time we called the police," said Tom. "We
need backup." He took out his phone and dialled
them.

"We need to find a way to hold the thieves until the police get here," said Kojo. "But how can we trap them?"

Sima thought hard. "I've got a plan," she said. "You'll need to make a hologram of me holding the diamond. Can you do that?"

"Sure," said Kojo, as he quickly created the hologram. "But I can't see how this is going to help at all."

"Listen and I will tell you," said Sima. She whispered her plan to the boys. Tom grinned.

"I like it!" he said. "I'll see you two in the vault in a few minutes."

Sima crept quietly into the back room and hid behind a pillar. At her signal, Kojo turned off all the holograms of the diamond in the open safe. The room went pitch black.

"What's going on?" snapped Jay.

"Don't know, Jay," said Joey.

"No idea," said Micky, scratching his head.

Just then, Kojo activated the hologram of Sima holding the diamond. It showed up in the doorway of the back room.

"Looking for this, guys?" called Sima from behind the pillar.

The thieves ran after the hologram. Kojo quickly relocated it to the top of the stairs that led down to the vault.

Sima kept well hidden in the shadows as she tailed the men out of the room.

Micky made a grab for the hologram, but Kojo now moved it to the bottom of the stairs.

HOW CAN SHE MOVE SO FAST? SHE'S LIKE AN ATHLETE!

WHATEVER! JUST GRAB THE STONE SO WE CAN GET OUT OF HERE.

8:00

The thieves ran as fast as they could down the stairs but Kojo quickly moved the hologram to inside the vault. The thieves ran right through the hologram and into the vault.

"What's going on?" shouted Micky. "This girl's see-through and I can't get hold of the diamond!"

"Nice try!" called Sima from outside the vault.

The men spun round and made a dash for the vault door, but Tom was too quick for them. He slammed the door shut and spun the lock as he looked at the men through the bars.

LOCKDOWN! THE POLICE WILL BE HERE ANY MOMENT NOW. I'M SURE THEY'LL BE ONLY TOO HAPPY TO LET YOU OUT.

Just then a bright light flashed and Sima, Tom and Kojo heard the words 'Game Over'. They shut their eyes tightly.

CHAPTER 5

The bright light faded and Sima, Tom and Kojo opened their eyes. They were back in the office.

"That was close," sighed Kojo. "As usual!"

"That was brilliant," said Tom. "The holograms were an amazing idea. Did you see the looks on their faces when those thieves realised they were trapped?"

Sima sat down and sighed. "I'm very glad that game's over," she said. "I don't ever want to see the Fire Diamond again."

"Oh really?" grinned Tom. "I thought you wanted to own one."

"Not any more," said Sima. "I'll stick with the crystal necklace you two gave me. That's far more valuable to me — and a lot less trouble!"

Glossary of terms

activate(d) make something active

autograph a signature, especially of someone famous

balaclava(s) a woollen covering of the whole head with gaps for eyes and mouth

CCTV closed circuit television

deploy(ed) use effectively

device(s) something that has been made to suit a particular purpose

disable(d) if you disable a piece of equipment you stop it from working properly

exhibition a display, e.g. of art, jewellery

fake not real

foolproof cannot be beaten

gallery a place where displays are set up for people to view

hologram a photograph which has three dimensions

laser(s) a piece of equipment that produces a narrow band of light

relocate(d) move to another place

vault a strongly protected room where valuables may be stored

Quiz

1 What sort of exhibiton did Sima, Tom and Kojo attend?

2 What was the name of Kojo's cousin?

3 What was the name of the special diamond?

4 In what part of the gallery did the game begin?

5 How many thieves were there altogether?

6 What were their names?

7 How did Kojo confuse the thieves about the true location of the diamond?

8 What did one of the thieves say Sima was like?

9 Where did Tom, Sima and Kojo trap the thieves?

10 How did Tom lock the door to the vault?

About the author

Sue Graves has taught for thirty years in Cheshire schools. She has been writing for more than ten years and has written well over a hundred books for children and young adults.

"Nearly everyone loves computer games. They are popular with all age groups — especially young adults. But I've often thought it would be amazing to play a computer game for real. To be in on the action would be the best experience ever! That's why I wrote these stories. I hope you enjoy reading them as much as I've enjoyed writing them for you."

ANSWERS TO QUIZ

1 Jewellery exhibition

2 Jasmine

3 The Fire Diamond

4 The security room at the City Gallery

5 Three

6 Jay, Micky and Joey

7 He put lots of holograms of the diamond in an open safe all around the walls

8 An athlete

9 In the vault

10 He spun the lock